SESAME STREET
GET READY
™

Ernie and Bert's Different Day

A Story About Opposites and Other Relational Concepts

By Andrew Gutelle

Illustrated by
Joe Ewers

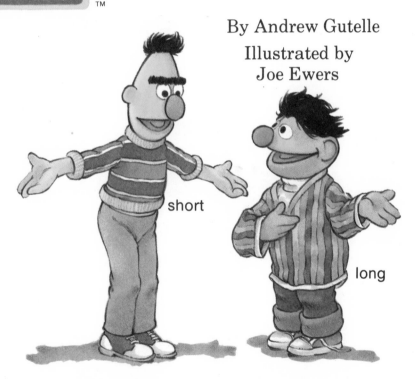

short

long

Featuring Jim Henson's Sesame Street Muppets

A Sesame Street/Golden Press Book

Published by Western Publishing Company, Inc., in conjunction
with Children's Television Workshop.

One morning when Bert was still **asleep** Ernie was **awake**. He had such a good idea that he couldn't wait a moment longer.

"Bert, old buddy, wake up!" Ernie said.

"Ernie! Why did you wake me up so early?" Bert yawned and rubbed his eyes.

"I have a great idea," said Ernie. "Today let's do everything in a different way! Won't that be fun, Bert?"

Bert did not think so. He liked to do the same things in the same way every day. But before Bert could answer, Ernie jumped out of bed to start his different day.

Later, Bert got up and went into the bathroom. He reached for his toothbrush, but it wasn't there.

"Ernie," called Bert, "where is my toothbrush?"

Ernie came to the door. "Where do you usually keep it?" he asked.

"**Over** the sink," said Bert.

"Today is different," said Ernie. "Today look **under** the sink for your toothbrush."

Bert sighed. Then he brushed his teeth and washed his face.

Bert went back into the bedroom. Ernie was already dressed. "Do you see anything different, Bert?" he asked.

"That's my shirt, Ernie!" said Bert.

"That's okay, Bert. You can wear mine," said Ernie.

Bert put on Ernie's shirt. "This is silly," he said. "This shirt is too **short** for me."

"Right, Bert," said Ernie. "And this shirt is too **long** for me!

"Come on. It's time for breakfast."

Ernie made toast for breakfast. He spread peanut
butter on it. Then he turned the toast over and took a
big bite. "Do you want a piece of upside-down toast,
Bert?" he asked.

"Now you're going too far, Ernie," said Bert. He poured some Toasted Oat Yummies into a bowl. "I'll have the same breakfast that I eat every day."

Bert's bowl was **full** of Toasted Oat Yummies with milk. He carefully ate every single one.

When he was finished, the bowl was **empty.**

After breakfast, it was time to clean up.

"I'll wash the dishes," said Ernie, and he ran to the sink.

"But that's my job," said Bert.

"Today is different!" said Ernie.

So Ernie washed the dishes, and Bert dried each one carefully.

"You're too **fast,** Ernie," said Bert.

"You're too **slow,**" said Ernie.

After the dishes were done, Ernie and Bert walked
to the park. Ernie ran right up to the sprinkler.
"Ernie, don't get too **near** that sprinkler," said
Bert. "I'm staying **far** away from it."

But Ernie ran through the sprinkler. "I'm being different, Bert!"

"Right," said Bert. "You're **wet,** and I'm **dry.**"

Then Ernie dashed over to the sandbox and
jumped in. "Look at me, Bert."

"Ernie, you're being silly," said Bert. "Now you're
dirty, and I'm still **clean.**"

Ernie and Bert decided it was time to swing.
Bert pumped and pumped as hard as he could.
Ernie let his legs dangle. He hardly moved at all.
"See, Bert? I'm swinging **low,** and you're swinging
high," said Ernie.

"Hey, Bert, I'm climbing **up** the slide," said Ernie.
"Now I'm climbing **down** the ladder."
"Ernie, that's no fun," said Bert.
"That's true, Bert," said Ernie. "But it's different!"

"Come on, Ernie!" called Bert. "It's time to go home."

"Okay, Bert," said Ernie. He followed his friend out of the playground. Bert walked **forward,** so Ernie walked **backward.**

As they walked
through the park
Ernie did
everything
differently from
Bert.

When Bert took
big steps, Ernie
took **little** ones.

When Bert walked **in front of** a park bench, Ernie
walked **behind** it.

When Bert walked **around** a pile of leaves, Ernie walked right **through** it!

Ernie stopped to buy some popcorn. There were
three sizes—**big, bigger,** and **biggest**. Ernie always
bought the biggest one for himself, but today was
different. So he bought the biggest cup for Bert.

"Ernie, I can't eat all this!" said Bert, looking down
at the mountain of popcorn.

"Don't worry, Bert," said Ernie. "I'll help you."
And he did.

"I'm very tired, Ernie," said Bert when they got home. "I'm going to relax and read the latest copy of *Pigeon News.*"

Bert turned **on** the reading light next to his easy chair.

"Bert, you keep forgetting about our different day!"
said Ernie. And he turned **off** the light.
"Errniee!" said Bert. "It's dark in here."

So Ernie turned the light back on.
"Now let's **open** all the windows in the
apartment," he said.
"It's too windy, Ernie," said Bert. "I want the
windows **closed.**"

At dinner Ernie put ice cubes in his vegetable soup.
"Today I will make my soup **cold,**" he said.
"I like my soup **hot,** Ernie," said Bert.

After dinner, Bert put away his toys. Then he watered the plants.

"I'll read you a story, Bert," said Ernie. "And they lived happily ever after," he read.

"Ernie!" cried Bert. "That's the **end** of the story, not the **beginning**."

"Right, Bert," said Ernie. "Once upon a time."

"I can't stand it anymore," said Bert. "I'm going to bed. Good night, Ernie."

"Good morning, Bert!"